More Time and Other Stories
Femdom Mind Control
Flash Fiction – Vol. 24

S.B.

Table of Contents

Give in always.

My sincerest thanks to all patrons of Spell... B-O-U-N-D for supporting my creativity.

Another Fun Night

Clark laid down the manuscript, tears rolling down his aquamarine eyes. That single piece of paper contained the most beautiful words he had ever read, and they were all his.

"When did I write this?" He looked at Darla, his Goddess, who sat by his side on the leather sofa, playing with an emerald pendant. They had only met six months ago, but it already felt like a lifetime, especially after she started hypnotizing him every single day after coming home from work. The call-center hours were insane, and the piled-up stress of having to deal with too many people who saw him as a robotic helper on the other end of the line and not a real person, even more. Drifting off for her was like awakening to a brand-new world every single time, one that was ripe with creative discoveries and fetish realizations he never believed possible.

"Last night, right here on this spot. You don't remember?" She replied, a strand of dark green hair falling over her sweet smile. Darla was a chameleon in human form, a woman of so many personalities that trying to count and understand them all would be a fool's errand. Back in her high school days, she collected boyfriends like they were stamps or coins but ever since leaving her twenties behind, she had come to realize real pleasure laid in having only the right person in her life, and he was it. Clark was twenty years older than her, but the age difference had never been a problem between them. If anything, it had only contributed to drawing them closer.

"No, I don't." He shrugged. Normally, he did, but sometimes, he fell so deep under her entrancing spell that everything else ceased to be, leaving behind nothing but an infinite wave of bliss.

"And isn't that hot?" She held the pendant slightly above his head, yet almost close enough to touch his wrinkled forehead.

"If you say so..."

"I do, and you love everything I say." The pendant swung from left to right and his weary gaze followed it.

"I... Can you tell me what else happened last night?"

"Hmm, so many delicious things..." She kissed his right earlobe, the pendant continuing to swing in and out of his drooping consciousness. "Do you want to experience some more?"

"I... I don't know." He nodded, speech getting slurred. "What if I don't remember again?"

"Then, I'll remember everything for you... and you'll love me even more."

"Hmmm..." He laid his head back against her wet, red-painted lips. "Is that even possible? I don't think it is..."

"That's why I get to do all the thinking around here..." She lowered the pendant even further, a single sparkle of light capturing his fluttering eyelids. "I speak and you obey."

"I obey..." The green pulled him under without resistance or complaint. He fell on her bosom, an empty vessel waiting to be filled by whatever suggestions she wanted to explore next. Having him write on command was amazing, but so was the striptease he had become so good at. Whoever said a fifty-year-old man didn't look good in a leopard thong had never met her beau. Darla smiled and took control of his mind again, starting with his hips. Another fun night for her to remember.

Ascension

Dana moaned atop the half-open bed as Alicia insinuated her lingerie-clad body against her ass, prodding fingers fighting a battle of supremacy against her laced purple panties and winning without effort. It felt so good, but even better was to hear her best friend's dulcet tones dripping inside her subconscious mind.

"That's it, sweetie, give in to your innermost desires. Let them fill you completely. You are a Goddess, the very definition of 'perfection'. You are a higher being that rightfully stands above all else. No man can ever satisfy you and please the divinity you carry within. No... you need something special, another woman's touch on your supple breasts... you need to feel her warm hands and eager tongue exploring your wet until you cum time and time again... You need another Goddess. You need me. Give in, now. Surrender to the truth you can no longer deny. You are a lesbian. You've always been a lesbian. You'll always be one for me."

Always? No. Far from it. It was a newfound revelation only made possible by Alicia's sweet hypnosis and brainwashing. Born into an exceedingly traditional family tainted by extreme religious views, Dana had spent most of her life believing that the only morally acceptable relationships were those between men and women, with the latter always playing second fiddle to their fat and lazy husbands no matter what. Anything that defied such a norm was not only vile, but the undeniable proof the devil walked among mortals, planting its seeds of doubt and confusion on all the weak souls he could find. Her father still believed in it, and so did her mother. What would both say if they say their only child succumbing to lust like that?

"Hmmm... yes, Goddess..." Dana licked her purple-painted lips, eyes rolling on the back of her head. The first time Alicia put her under, she felt nothing but a low-key buzz on her aching soul, but now each repetition triggered an almost immediate orgasmic response she couldn't shake off even if she wanted to. Resistance was for fools, and she chose to be smart. She had to sink and accept.

"Good." Alicia continued, so proud of her evolution over the last couple of weeks. The shy and demure mid-twenties woman was growing to become a force to be reckoned with, her ultimate ascension almost complete. The oppressive shackles of her misguided parents were almost gone, melting away in the bliss of surrender.

"Deeper now. Fall into my words, for they are yours, too. Your mind and your thoughts mirror my own. Your voice is an extension of mine. You've been fed lies since forever, my dear. Men are not your superiors. They're not even fit to be your equals. They do not deserve to be on the same level as you. See them for what they are, with the eyes of a conqueror. They are but sacks of flesh, mere tools for your divinity... Take them. Use them. Own them. Do with them as you please, and without holding back. That is your divine right. They're all yours now, just like you're all mine."

Dana nodded mindlessly as a ringed finger pushed deep inside her snatch and lingered there, perpetuating the pleasure she now knew she deserved. Lesbian. Goddess. Hers. All would kneel before them in agony and delight.

Don't Move

Please stay still. You've just stepped on a live hypnotic mine. Any sudden movement and you'll obliterate the free will of everyone in this park and all the surrounding blocks. I know it's a lot to process right now, but the good news is that I can defuse it. You'll be fine if you do what I say. Don't move.

Okay. Good. You must have a million things going on in your mind, but don't let this be one of them, okay? It's not your fault. You're not responsible for what's happening. If anything, it's the government that's to blame. They know there are still hundreds of these scattered everywhere, but they chose to keep the information from the public to avoid panic. Joke's on them now, I say. The public opinion will crucify them when they hear about this. Honestly, I can't wait.

I hope I'm not bothering you with this. If I am, I apologize, but that's how I deal with this stuff. Some people prefer complete silence to remain focused, but not me. I ramble, for that's the only way my mind can go into autopilot to work through this. You're doing great, by the way. Just hold that position, please. Last week, I was in a similar predicament and the person stepping on the mine let go of the foot before I gave the order. I thought we were all goners then but, strangely, it didn't explode. I don't know why that was, but we better not push our luck, right?

Hey, did you just shiver? Shit! I probably shouldn't have told you that story, huh? Please, don't do that again. Your muscles need to be perfectly still. Can you do that for me?

Hmm, I know. Let's try something that might help. There's a statue of a man reading a book in front of you. It's one of my favorites. Did you know it's been here since the day this park opened to the public? Probably not. I want you to look at it, okay? Look at the statue and nothing but the statue. Focus on the fact that nothing disturbs it. Whether it's raining or snowing, whether there are birds pooping on it or people leaning against it to take a selfie, it never budges, never compromises. It's always there, in perpetual rest, immobile, frozen, unafraid. Now, think how much you want to be like that, how you need to remain still, all your emotions at ease while you listen to my voice... only my voice... my voice telling you to be like that statue, your mind acknowledging that if you do that, you and everyone else will be safe. Calm... still... statues don't think... statues have no worries... statues have no fears... yes...

Good job. Keep being a statue, frozen in place so I can do my work. Now, let me just check this and this... perfect! You did it. The mine is harmless, now. You can wake up from your trance in 3, 2, 1...

Hello? I said you could snap out of it now. You no longer need to do this. Hello? Can you hear me?

Well... look who's loving this feeling and doesn't want to let go. It was only a light trance to keep you at ease, but you love it just a little too much, don't you? You love falling deeper and deeper, losing yourself completely to my words and suggestions... and you know what? That's hot!

So... since you're so receptive and suggestible, let me fill you in on a secret. Even though it is my job to dispose of them, I really love hypnotic mines. I would never hypnotize and enslave so many people like those terrorists, but one or two now and then? A mindless toy for me to use? Yeah, I've had a few, and I guess now it's your turn. Listen closely, my little statue. I have big plans for you this weekend. This will be fun.

Everything You Are

How cute, you still think you're capable of resisting me... you still believe you're your own person. I've seen this happen before, time and time again, but not to this extent. You're still convinced I haven't turned your world upside down, huh?

Okay, boy. Let me be clear about this. Everything you believe in today is a lie, a fabrication of my design. I control every single aspect of your existence, and I've been doing it for ages now. I dictate your schedule, what you eat, the clothes you wear, the books you read, the movies you watch... absolutely everything, and that's the truth!

Impossible? You would know? You did once. Before you came to me, you still had free will, and your perception of reality wasn't so fucked up, but now you're in too deep, the neural pathways are fully formed. You can't escape my dominion even if you wanted to, and you don't. You don't want to do anything other than what I tell you to do, so, for instance, if I say "Sleep" ...

(...)

... and wake up. Welcome back. What did you think of the last half hour? Do you remember anything of it? Of course, you don't. I told you not to and your mind automatically complied, for it knows who's the boss. Feels wonderful, doesn't it? Having no choice is the best feeling in the world.

Hmm, not convinced yet, I see. Okay, then. So, if I say the word "Red" ...

(...)

Ah, you look like a pepper, dear. The color doesn't flatter you at all, but I love it, so you'll be wearing it for the rest of the week. Shh, not a word... trying to complain is both foolish and annoying. I already told you, your fate is sealed! It's all right here, see? You signed the contract willingly, and now you're mine. Body and soul. And if I want just a part of you, that's what you'll be. Now, listen carefully... "Cock."

(...)

Hmmm, yes... just like that! Real men fuck real women with real cocks, but puppets like you are lucky to even get to use a plastic one. Harder now. You'll be used in any way I see fit, slave boy, and then you'll forget until I need you again. Speaking of which, it's that time again. Fuck and forget. Fuck... and forget.

Fading Away

Trevor rose from bed and checked his surroundings. They looked strange, yet familiar, as if he had slipped into a parallel dimension overnight.

Perhaps he did. The last thing he remembered was talking to his stepsister, Roxanne, over a glass of red wine. She had always been the weird one, fascinated with crystals, numerology, mirrors and...

... Hypnosis?

Vague impressions of their last conversation swirled in his mind... something about how pretty her eyes were under a candlelight. He nodded silently, more focused on her cleavage than anything else and then...

Darkness... her voice echoing in the distance... fingers snapping once, twice...

A dream? He had a lot of those, more than he could remember. They were bizarre affair, filled with disjointed imagery, like lights flashing in erratic succession over his eyes and...

He was doing it again, losing track of thoughts and things he wanted to say. But say it to whom? There was no one with him in the bedroom, not even his own shadow. He stood on the fluffy carpet, head facing the only exit of the bedroom but not really wanting to leave. It all felt so...

... pointless.

"Okay, what are you saying?" He chastised himself, trying to push the numbness away. "Go back a little. Go back to..."

... the dinner from the night before... Roxanne smiling in her low-cut mini dress. Was it red? Blue? Something in-between? It matched the unnatural color of her eyes under the candlelight when things got blurry. She...

... kissed him. On the neck, on his lips, on the tip of his cock. She kissed him eagerly as he stood to attention, not moving a muscle, every part of him frozen under her watchful eye, just like he was doing right now.

He blinked, and the room wobbled, a reflection of a memory trying to push through. This wasn't real! It was some sort of mental projection, a dream within a dream to keep him calm, sedated, compliant.

"Wake up, now!" He pinched himself, but there was no sensation of touch, no pain, no nothing. He looked down and gasped to see that his naked feet weren't even touching the floor.

"What? No! This is... this..."

The memories folded into themselves, cracking holes in everything he thought he knew. The dinner... Roxanne... her eyes under the candlelight...

What were they talking about?

Money. Of course! It was always about money with her. She never paid for her extravaganzas when she could have others do it for her. And he always paid. He always obeyed her when she kissed him like that, and her honeyed lips and eyes became his sole purpose for existence. He couldn't live without her. He wouldn't live without her.

Trevor glanced at the bed and saw his body lying there, glassy eyes and purplish lips, poisoned by her suggestions, empty wallet between his legs. She always got what she wanted, even his life if he were ever to become useless, and it had finally happened. No tears, no remorse. There were plenty more fish at sea.

Unable to process another thought, he floated in limbo, waiting to fade away.

Fun Times

The once creepy crawler climbed on the back of Thomas' left hand, its furry legs giving him the tickles. He had been afraid of spiders all his life after he had been bitten by one when he was only three. Now, on the eve of his twenty-seventh birthday, it was as if all those years of uncontrolled phobia had been nothing but a series of bad dreams he was ready to forget.

"Oh fuck, this is amazing!"

"It certainly is." Patricia nodded in agreement. She couldn't be prouder of his progress, especially after the first couple of days when it seemed like the universe was collapsing all around and there was nothing,he could do to stop it.

"I can't believe this is really happening." He smiled at the tarantula who was clearly enjoying having yet another human to explore to its heart's content.

"You better believe it. Well done!"

"I didn't do a thing. If you hadn't hypnotized me…" He blushed.

"… it wouldn't have worked if you weren't willing to accept the change, dear. You conquered your fear, but you still haven't unlocked your true potential. Want to keep going?"

"And do what?"

"Whatever you want. Just say the word and I'm here for you, no matter what."

"Thank you. Oh, thank you. Thank you!" He rushed to kiss her cheeks.

"What? No lips?" She teased him with a taste of tongue on his right earlobe.

"Can I?"

"You can do whatever you set your mind to. What are you thinking about right now?"

"I... I think I want to keep him as a pet..." He brushed his fingers against the spider's back. "... but I know nothing about taking care of one though."

"They're not that hard, I'll gladly teach you everything there is to know if you really want to go through with this."

"Yes. Yes, I do."

"Congratulations, you just got yourself a new pet!"

"Wait until my brothers hear about this. They're going to lose their minds!"

"I bet. You're a wonderful subject, one of the best I ever had."

"Are you serious?"

"When have I ever lied to you?"

Never, as far he knew. Then again, the hypnotic conditioning around his mind was so strong he wouldn't be able to know for sure. As he sat there with his new companion now cuddling around his neck and her violet eyes locked on his, he couldn't help but think how lucky he was. Until the day he had heard her casually talk about how much she loved hypnosis, Patricia had always been nothing but a distant co-worker he only dreamed of flirting with. Fate had brought them together in and out of trance, and their love just kept on blooming.

"This is the best birthday present ever."

"That's good to hear. Can I have one of my own?"

"Of course! Anything you want!"

"Anything?" She smirked.

"Yes!"

"Then, how about...?" She whispered gently, making his cock hard without even trying.

"Oh... and you're sure that will work?"

"Positive!"

"If you believe it, then so do I. Let's go for it."

"Right now?"

"Yeah, and we can buy some stuff for this guy while we're at it."

"Lead the way."

Their afternoon excursion first took them to a pet store and then to the largest sex shop in town. The surprises were never-ending and so was her figure in a tight latex dress. Only fun times ahead.

Identical

Anthony looked at the picture to the left and then at the one on the right. He squinted, trying to figure out what exactly Samantha was trying to show him, but to no avail. Was this another one of her jokes?

"I don't get it." He confronted his girlfriend, who was happily playing with her phone. "They're absolutely identical."

"Are they really?" She asked, caressing her purple-painted lips with a solitary finger. Of all the little flirtatious gestures she pulled off effortlessly, that was his favorite, a real gem.

"Yes. Of course, they are."

"Okay then." She laid down the phone on the sofa and snatched both pictures from his sweaty palms. "Thank you for your cooperation. That is all for today."

"Huh?"

"It's over, baby. You can go back to your video games or whatever it is you do in your man-cave."

"Not until you tell me what this was all about."

"This what?" She let out a mysterious grin.

"This; Sam! Having me stare at the same picture for the last twenty minutes! What gives?"

"Oh, it's nothing special, really."

"When you say that, you always mean the opposite." He stretched his fingers, felt the knuckles crack. "Tell me what's going on."

"Fine. If you insist, I was just testing a theory."

"And that theory is...?"

"You only see what I want you to see now." She held the pictures again before his eyes, the dark outlines in each one becoming more pronounced.

"You're losing me again."

"No, sweetie. I'm winning you over more and more with each breath you take. Still think they're the same picture?"

"Yes… because they are!"

Samantha reached for his forehead and planted a single kiss there, momentarily snapping him from the altered state of mind he had been drifting in for over an hour. He blinked heavily, shallow breath returning to normal.

"And now?" She insisted.

Anthony gasped as the true nature of the pictures revealed itself. On her left hand, she held a copy of Salvador Dali's *The Persistence of Memory*. On the right, Edvard Munch's *The Scream* had him shudder.

"Oh, shit!"

"You see what I want you to see, remember what I want you to remember, and do what I want you to do. Remember when you told me I could never control you completely?"

"No."

"Exactly. Go along, now. My work is done."

"I..." He nodded his head in utter disbelief. "I... don't feel like playing anything anymore."

"In that case..." Her lips touched his, and he melted again, thoughts filled with the need to make her happy, no matter the cost. Soon, his name and the word "slave" would be identical in his mind.

More Time

Dawn of The First Day - 72 Hours Remain

Lance opened his eyes and jumped out of bed. 6 am. Mistress Mona had a gigantic list of chores waiting for him. His service to her was all. She would not be denied.

He took a quick shower, had breakfast, and then walked to her house. Ever since she had ordered him to sell his car to pay for her next vacations, he exercised every day and had already lost fifteen pounds. It wouldn't be surprising to shed a few more during the long weekend ahead.

When he arrived there, he performed the customary ritual of kissing her booted feet three times and then immediately got to work. He cleaned up the attic, the kitchen, and the bathroom before switching all the furniture in the living-room.

At lunch time, he ate a sandwich and then moved to the BDSM studio, which needed a new coat of paint. The discovery of a recent water leak in one wall had him check the plumbing first, so the work got delayed. He still had half of the studio to complete when the sun went down and, without natural light, continuing was a fool's errand. Before leaving for the night, he switched clothes, got her some last-minute groceries, and replaced a faulty light bulb. Good work, but far from finished. Then he walked home alone, eyeing the full moon up high. It was almost as if was grinning at him.

He fell asleep right after hitting the bed, dreaming only of her will.

Dawn of The Second Day - 48 Hours Remain

Lance opened his eyes and jumped out of bed. One minute earlier than the day before, the remaining chores on the list never leaving the back of his mind. He rushed to her place and finished work on the studio before heading outside. There was grass to mow, hedges to trim, flower beds to replant. The crescent-shaped pool required cleaning, the garage door mechanism had to be replaced, and then there was the matter of clearing out all the ivy creeping up the walls. Time moved so quickly he didn't even see it, focused only on her pleasure.

Still, it wasn't enough. Minutes turned to hours, red, orange, and yellow covered the sky once more. Could he really finish everything in time? He had to! Mistress would be disappointed if he didn't, so he kept pushing himself past the limits of exhaustion, and the unthinkable happened.

She found him curled on the porch at 8 pm. A five-minute break to rest his eyes and weary muscles had turned into a two-hour nap but, instead of feeling revitalized when he woke up, he was even more drained following her scolding. He was sent away without the chance to kiss her boots again, aware that if he failed her again the next day it was all over.

The moon shone its dying light on his teary face. It was getting closer. There was no time to waste.

Dawn of The Final Day - 24 Hours Remain

Lance opened his eyes and jumped out of bed. 6:37 am. Shit! He was already late and if she reprimanded him again... He had breakfast on the road and ran to get to her. Despite his best efforts, he was still twenty minutes late and there were now more items on the list. He had to walk to the other side of the city to buy food for her dogs, then wax her car, polish two wardrobes of latex outfits, spit shine fifty pair of boots...

It was too much! The clock was speeding up, the music in his mind getting out of control. 24/7 slavery was exhausting, but he couldn't stop. He met her in the music studio and begged for forgiveness.

"I need more time, Goddess! Please, I need more time."

"You know what to do then." Mistress Mona pointed at the piano in the center of the room. "Go for it."

He crawled to the instrument and played a series of familiar notes from his childhood. Almost instantly, he drifted into mindless trance as the memories of all his recent accomplishments faded away. Blank-eyed, he waited for the cycle to start anew in his mind.

Mistress Mona smirked and patted him on the head before sending him back to his place, completely oblivious to everything. He didn't have to worry about remembering a thing, for she did it for him. She never got enough of this scene, and neither did he. He had no choice. Who knew that having a hypnoslave that was also a *Legend of Zelda* fan could be so much fun?

Once a Cuck…

Marcus stood by Amy's bed, naked, spiked cock cage burrowing deep against his manhood. His hands were shaking uncontrollably, and he had blood in his eyes, an angry pawn trying to break free from a cycle of violence and abuse.

He had loved her since they were teenagers, and even then, she had shown him nothing but contempt. He did her homework, carried her books around, allowed her to cheat on exams, never worried about the possible consequences to himself. When drugs were found in her locker during their senior year, he stepped forward to take the blame. Love made him blind, the insidious brainwashing did the rest.

After he was released, he still hung around her, desperate for attention, willing to sacrifice everything to make her happy. While he dreamed of being her boyfriend, she saw nothing in him except a crybaby loser with 'beta type' slapped in his forehead. Hundreds of sultry smiles and hidden commands later, and he was completely hers, locked above and below. When he was not working to make her money, he cleaned her house, did her shopping, washed her car... everything she wanted and more, reduced to utmost silence in her presence, ashamed to even be breathing the same air as a living Goddess.

It all changed when Derek came into the picture. The early twenties basketball player was the opposite of him: tall, well-built, huge cock. Sometimes, she sucked him hard and made him watch, and there was nothing worse than watching the face of the woman he loved covered in his cum. No more. No fucking more!

Derek laid beside her, his dick rock solid. He was probably dreaming of fucking her again. The nerve! "Dream of this, asshole!" He spat, suddenly raising a serrated knife.

"What do you think you're doing, bitch boy?" Amy opened her eyes and smiled, evilly, at him. "Hey, baby, check this out!"

Her lover grumbled and sat in bed, laughing, upon noticing how ridiculous Marcus looked, holding a blade at least ten times larger than his micro-penis. "Seriously, bro?"

"Thanks for the laugh, bitch, but you better put that down before someone gets hurt." Amy commanded.

"No! You ruined my life. I'm done, you hear? You're right, someone will get hurt and it won't be me anymore!" He jumped onto the bed, frantically waving the knife until her scream froze him in his tracks.

"ENOUGH! What's this all about now? Oh, right... you're jealous of this, aren't you?" She grabbed Derek's cock and grinned. "You want what you can never have, but I know just the thing to keep you focused again. How about you take it in your mouth and apologize for acting out like an idiot?"

"No!"

"Too bad you don't have a choice, you little mindfucked toy. Drop the knife and do it now."

"No!"

"I said: NOW! Slaves obey. You will follow my orders."

"Yeah, bitch..." Derek stretched his tattooed arms around his back. "Feast yourself and gain some sense. Once a cuck..."

"... always a cuck." Marcus mumbled, tears rolling down his cheeks. The knife landed on the satin sheets as his mind fell into degrading captivity once more.

Painless

Daniel Silver was a man of many flaws but being late for an appointment was not one of them. However, more than a boon, his famed British punctuality had been a source of many embarrassing situations in the past like the time he caught his boss fucking his secretary doggy-style atop the Conference Room's table and then had to make a presentation ten minutes later while looking at a poorly cleaned cum stain. A few others had followed, all involving sex, but none as bizarre as what happened on Good Friday.

He had agreed to meet his brother at 4 pm, outside his doctor's office. Jonah claimed it was time for his annual check-up, but he knew better. Dr. Harris was a woman of many talents with the most beautiful pair of tits he had seen. The younger sibling of the Silver family was after something more than a professional relationship, but whether he would get it or not, no one knew.

Daniel arrived at the office almost twenty minutes before schedule and was surprised to find it empty. Even the doctor's secretary was nowhere to be seen. A sepulchral silence spread from the entrance's glass doors to the rooms beyond. Driven by a morbid curiosity, he walked in. It was then he heard giggles coming from an open door at the back. He approached it soundlessly and peeked inside.

Dr. Harris and her secretary stood next to one another, fondling a third woman atop a vintage hospital metal gurney. She was a natural blonde and completely naked, legs spread apart, and shaved pussy stretched by gloved fingers too eager to humiliate her. The woman's face was all too familiar, even though he had never seen her before.

Befuddled, and more aroused than he cared to admit, he remained transfixed watching the medical debauchery go down. A Wartenberg wheel connected to a violet wand slid across the young woman's legs and she moaned, losing herself to the blissful pleasure only her Mistress and her favorite toy could provide. Next thing he knew, he was scrambling to hold his cock, feeling the need to stroke to the three beauties as soon as possible.

"If you insist on doing that, at least do it where we can all see you." Dr. Harris suddenly said, taking him by surprise. Daniel lost his balance and fell inside the office, fly wide open, boxers slightly pulled down.

"Hey, Daniel." The naked sex slave looked at him and smiled. "What are you doing here so early?"

"Friend of yours?" Dr. Harris stopped playing with her pussy and crossed her arms.

"My brother. He's a good guy but always has a stick up his ass. You know what would be great, Mistress? If you did to him the same thing you did to me..."

"Hmmm... I like that." The secretary said with a smirk. "Can we, Mistress? Please!"

"I don't see why not." The Dr. crouched next to the embarrassed man, endless magical spirals swirling in her eyes. "What do you say, brother? Want to join in on the fun?"

"What is going on here?" He grumbled, eyes locked on her as a veil of tiredness fell over his shoulders. "Where is Jonah?"

"Right here, and it's Joan now, silly. Haven't you been paying attention? Worry not, the transformation is painless, and you'll love every second... just like I did."

The spirals engulfed the whole room and Daniel plunged into an abyss of magic where everything impossible was real. By the time the light died down, only Danielle remained, and she was quite the slut. She joined her sister on the gurney, another obedient pet for eternity.

Sweet Death

The upside-down reflection on her apartment's bathroom mirror demanded Gina's attention and utter compliance.

"You need to touch yourself." It purred. *"Do it now."*

"No!" The brunette police detective clenched her teeth and gasped. "I won't! I won't succumb!"

"You must." Her twisted doppelganger insisted, crimson lipstick blowing her a kiss. *"You have no choice. Pleasuring yourself will make Agnes happy, and you want to please her. You need to please her so badly. You will please her tonight."*

"I already said no!" Gina let out a piercing shriek, but the sharp tones weren't loud enough to break the glass nor the mental prison she was trapped in.

Agnes Williamson, a.k.a. Sweet_Death in the Los Angeles underground scene was a former low-life dealer with bleached hair and more piercings a normal human ear could handle that had suddenly risen to prominence following the appearance of a new narcotic in the market. Not much was known about it - it didn't have a real street name yet! - but rumors talked about permanent brain injuries and complete personality rewrites derived from "ultra-realistic hallucinogenic states". For Gina, who had always been an adamant skeptic, words like that were just tell-tales to scare the unwary. The only things she believed in were justice and retribution... until she was exposed.

She knew not where. Perhaps outside Agnes' flat when a crazy biker nearly ran her over; perhaps at the rave downtown following a lead that led nowhere... she didn't feel the needle, but the side effects were already out of control, projecting wicked sexual desires onto her psyche.

"Agnes is your Goddess. Doing whatever she wants is what you crave the most. Start slow, Gina. One finger up your cunt just enough to get it all wet and then another you can take to your lips and let the ecstasy pour in. Obey. You need to obey your owner."

"GET. OUT. OF. MY. HEAD!" Gina spun by the sink, trembling fingers pressed against her temples. Her eyes were becoming glassy, warm blood dripping from her nasal cavities.

"You head is mine now and I'm never leaving it alone. Not until you give in. Endless pleasure for a simple act of obedience, Gina. Don't you want to be a good girl for your owner?"

"I... no... yes... fuck!" Gina moaned. Her pussy was so warm, she could feel its fluids building up under the dark blue linen pants. Her phone laid on the floor, one button press away from calling for help. She just had to...

"Don't bother, dear. 911 can't save you now. No one can. No one except Agnes, the most powerful woman that ever lived. Her sweet death gives you structure and purpose.

Let her take you to where you need to be. Obey. Obey her now!"

"Damn it!" Gina drooled as her upper limbs finally betrayed her. She lowered her pants, banged her head against the ceramic white tiles, and pushed two fingers as hard as she could inside her tight slit.

"Do it for Agnes and lose yourself." The imaginary nemesis grinned as Gina's consciousness and resistance slowly faded into black. A new addict in the making, one more slave waiting to be born. She would be the first female agent turned mindless drone at the dealer's service, but certainly not the last.

What a Bargain!

Danielle loaded the New Amazonian's Movement Slave Services website and fumed when she was greeted by another blank screen.

"Down again? Oh, for fuck's sake! What are you doing?" She resisted the temptation of smashing her laptop's screen.

It was the third time in the last week, a far cry from the 24/7 service promised, and now she had to do the one thing she hated the most: talk to another person. Still trying to keep her wits together, Danielle called the hotline and waited to be transferred to an operator.

"NAM's Slave Services. This is Jane speaking. How may I help you?"

"Good evening, Citizen Jane. I've tried to order a slave online, but your site is not working. I'm hoping you can register the order for me."

"Certainly. It will be my pleasure. Apologies for the downtime, but we're in the middle of a major renovation with some services being more affected than others. Before we proceed, may I please ask for your retinal verification scan?"

"Yes, of course." Danielle held the phone to her right eye for five seconds without blinking as the bio-metrical data was authenticated.

"Thank you, Citizen Danielle. Your identity has been verified, and the information on the global servers is synced with ours. I will now ask you a series of questions to determine what type of slave you're interested in. The first question is: temporary or permanent?"

"Temporary, please. I'm having a party this coming weekend, and I'm short on the entertainment side."

"Very well." Jane took notes as they went along. "Will you be requiring any special entertainment skills then?"

"Being a good stripper is a must, obviously."

"Of course. Penis size preference? We have all lengths available right now, including a rare twelve-inches from the latest batch."

"Twelve inches? Nah, that's overkill! Between seven and eight is fine, really."

"Understood. Just a few more questions please, and then I can process your order."

The remaining ones were the boring kind that made any real woman shrug and yawn. Skin tone, color of the eyes, shape of the nose and ears, type of jawline... who cared about any of that shit? Slaves weren't real people no matter the personalization options included, and it's not like she or any of the guests would look at his face, anyway. Zoning out, she checked the most common options and even allowed the operator to select a few.

"Can you please hurry, Citizen Jane? This is getting annoying."

"Apologies once more, Citizen Danielle, but I'm contractually obliged to tell you all about the new tattoo designs added to our catalog last month. I've just sent a few samples to your phone. Can you please tell me your favorites, if any?"

"I don't have any. I'm not interested, okay? I just want my slave a.s.a.p. If I could have it first thing in the morning, that would be great."

"That is certainly possible but, because of the delicate nature of our work, any order fulfilled in under 24 hours, will have a 30% Additional Charge plus taxes, of course. Is that okay? May I proceed?"

"Please do. Thank you."

"You're most welcome, Citizen Danielle. I'm now processing the details of your order. You should receive the info right about... now.

The pink phone's screen lit up, all elements of the transaction fully discriminated: Male - obviously! - Caucasian, six feet one, jet-black hair, green eyes, perky smile, 8-inches cock, enhanced stripping skills, no tats, or any visible scars. Everything was perfect.

"It all checks out. Thank you once again." Danielle stretched her arms. The longest twenty minutes of her life were finally over.

"Happy to have been of service. Your new temporary slave is scheduled to be delivered at your doorstep at 8 am sharp, Citizen Danielle. As always, you have twenty-hours to inspect and test it as well as report any programming glitches you encounter. As of March 31st of the current year, our failure rate is 0,027%. Have a good day."

Danielle hung up and checked the site again. Still down, but the worst was gone. The waiting game never bothered her, just the dumb questions. She slid into the kitchen, opened a beer bottle, and resumed the party's preparations.

Meanwhile, deep underground, Clone 326854/D9 was removed from its stasis chamber and dragged to the Slave Service's Laboratory for both physical and mental programming. It had only been 'alive' for about an hour, and everything about it was malleable. It had no memories, but soon, it would be the greatest stripper ever for only $3000 plus tax. What a bargain!

About the author

S.B., Simple Being, middle name Creative. Writer and artist with a penchant for themes of Femdom Hypnosis and Mind Control. His thoughts are his own except when they're not.

Besides indulging himself in kinky delights, he loves his furry family of two (dogs), sci-fi and horror stories, and puns galore. He's also been writing a piece of erotic micro-fiction every single day since January 1st, 2016 and has no intention of stopping anytime soon.

Find out more and keep up with his latest extravaganzas by visiting and supporting his personal website, Spell… B-O-U-N-D.

www.ingramcontent.com/pod-product-compliance
Lightning Source LLC
Chambersburg PA
CBHW060921130726

48001CB00006B/2347